To all the loving dads out there:
Jacob, Herb, Peter, Mike,
my dad, Jimmy,
and your dad, _____
—G.C.

For Jodi
—D.S.

G. P. PUTNAM'S SONS
an imprint of Penguin Random House LLC
375 Hudson Street, New York, NY 10014

Library of Congress Cataloging-in-Publication Data
Names: Choldenko, Gennifer, 1957– | Santat, Dan, illustrator.
Title: Dad and the dinosaur / Gennifer Choldenko ; illustrated by Dan Santat.
Description: New York, NY : G. P. Putnam's Sons, [2017]
Summary: "A boy keeps a toy dinosaur in his pocket to help him be brave like his dad—but
when the dinosaur goes missing, Dad knows just what to do"—Provided by publisher.
Identifiers: LCCN 2016009819 | ISBN 9780399243530 (hardback)
Subjects: | CYAC: Toys—Fiction. | Dinosaurs—Fiction. | Fear—Fiction. | Fathers and sons—Fiction.
| BISAC: JUVENILE FICTION / Family / Parents. | JUVENILE FICTION / Animals / Dinosaurs &
Prehistoric Creatures. | JUVENILE FICTION / Social Issues / Emotions & Feelings.
Classification: LCC PZ7.C446265 Dad 2017 | DDC [E]—dc23
LC record available at https://lccn.loc.gov/2016009819

Manufactured in China
ISBN 9780399243530
1 3 5 7 9 10 8 6 4 2

Design by Ryan Thomann. Text set in Drawzing.
The art was created with pencil, watercolor, ink, acrylic, and Photoshop.

DAD
AND THE
DINOSAUR

NEWBERY HONOR WINNER
GENNIFER CHOLDENKO

CALDECOTT AWARD WINNER
DAN SANTAT

G. P. PUTNAM'S SONS

Nicholas was afraid of the dark outside his door, the bushes where the giant bugs lived, and the undersides of manhole covers.

His dad was not afraid of anything.

Nicholas tried to be brave like his dad, but he needed help . . . big help.
He needed a dinosaur.

Dinosaurs like the dark, bugs are nothing to them, and they eat manhole covers for lunch and everything under them for dinner.

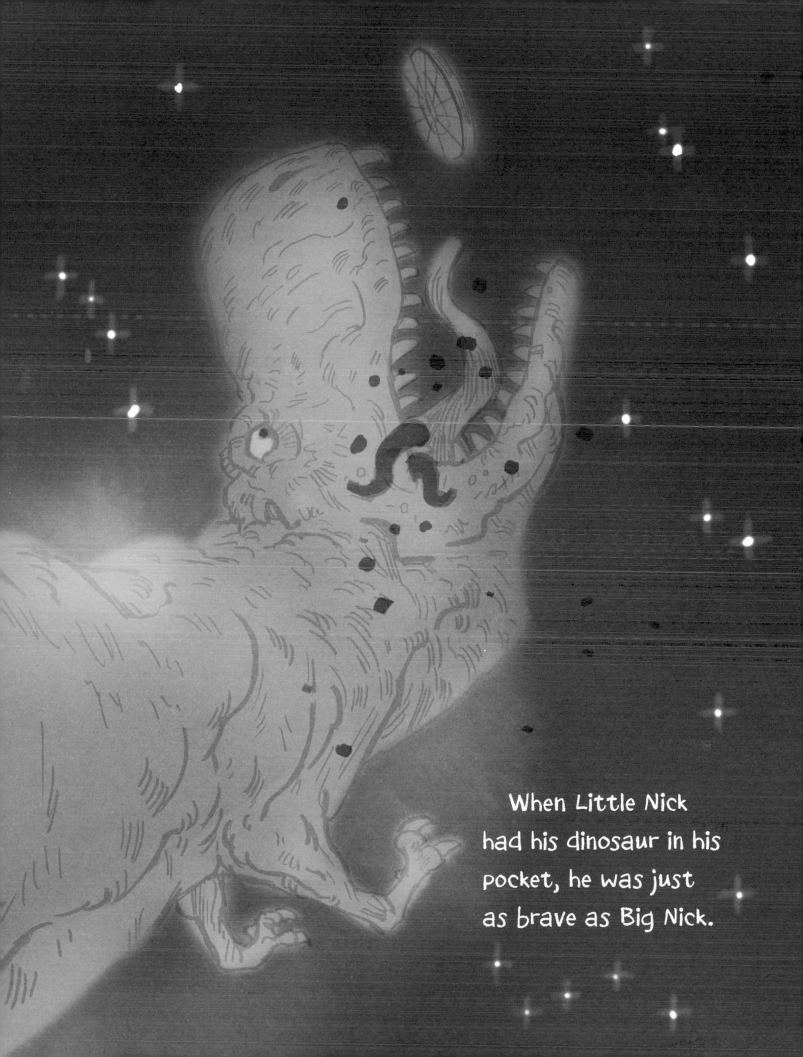

When Little Nick
had his dinosaur in his
pocket, he was just
as brave as Big Nick.

"You should have seen your son at the climbing wall today," his mom told his dad.

"No fear at all.
He takes after **your** side
of the family."

Of course, there were times when Nicholas had no pockets.

During soccer, he hid his dinosaur in his sock.

When he swam, he tied the dinosaur to the cord of his swim trunks.

At night, his dinosaur went under the pillow.

Then one day at soccer, Nicholas played against the goalie they called Gorilla. But no worries. Nicholas had his dinosaur and his dinosaur was fearless. He kicked the ball so hard it shot past Gorilla's oven-mitt-size hands straight into the net.

Everybody cheered!

His mom had the
whole thing on video.

"You're incredible,
buddy," Big Nick told him.

Nicholas's face lit up
like a glow stick.

But when it was time to
leave, the dinosaur was gone.

Nicholas searched from one
end of the field to the other,
until it grew dark.

"What are you doing, Nick?"

"Nothing," Nicholas said.

On the way home, the night
was as black as octopus ink, giant bugs
were everywhere, and their little car
was nearly sucked under the street.

Nicholas ate no dinner that night.
He went to sleep early with the light on
and nothing under his pillow.

He dreamed about bugs as
big as buildings and the world
under the manhole cover.

When his father got home late that night,
he came into Little Nick's room. "You have a bad
dream, buddy?" he asked.

Nicholas didn't answer.

"It's okay to be afraid. All guys are now and then."

"Who said I was afraid?" Nicholas shot back.

"Nobody," Dad said. "But something's the matter."

After a long time, Nicholas whispered,
"I lost my dinosaur. He's the brave one.
Not me."

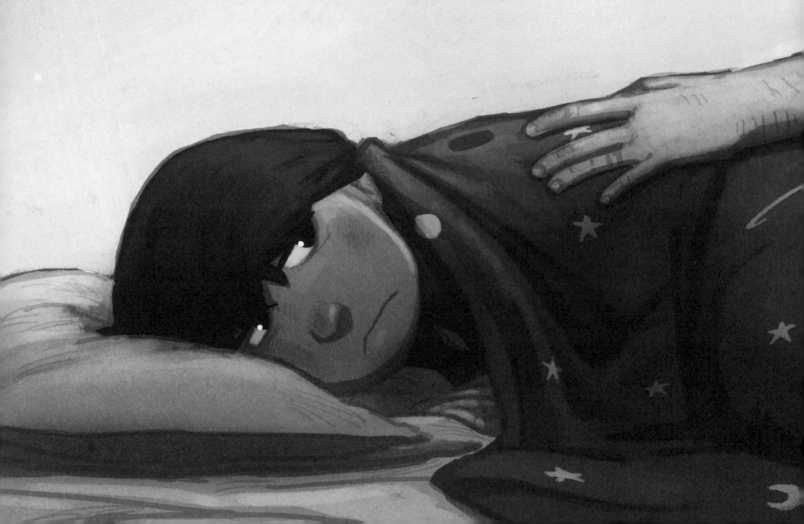

"Let's go
find him, then,"
Dad said.

His mother heard them
putting on their jackets.
"Where are you two going
at this hour?"

"It's guy stuff,"
his father answered as
they walked out the door.

Dad drove Nicholas across town
to the dark field. Together they
searched the spongy grass.

Sure enough, there
was Nicholas's dinosaur,
as big as ever.

When they got home, they
gave the dinosaur a bath and
put him under the pillow.

"Dad?" Nicholas said.
"Don't tell Mom, okay?"

"Course not," Dad said.

The next day, Nicholas put
his dinosaur in his pocket.

But he wasn't
the only one who
knew he was there.